KATIE KAZOO, SWITCHEROO

# No Messin' with My Lesson

For my parents, Gladys and Steve—N.K.

For Julia Andrews—J&W

ISBN-13: 978-0-545-11375-5
ISBN-10: 0-545-11375-X

12 11 10 9 8                    12 13/0

Printed in the U.S.A.          40

First Scholastic printing, September 2008

# No Messin' with My Lesson

by Nancy Krulik • illustrated by John & Wendy

## SCHOLASTIC INC.

New York  Toronto  London  Auckland  Sydney
Mexico City  New Delhi  Hong Kong  Buenos Aires

# Chapter 1

"Cinderella, dressed in yellow. Went upstairs to kiss a fella. Made a mistake, and kissed a snake. How many doctors did it take? One, two, three . . ."

Katie Carew began to count as she turned her end of the double Dutch jump ropes. Her best friend, Suzanne Lock, was jumping between the ropes. Becky Stern was turning the other end.

Katie's other best friend, Jeremy Fox, was on the soccer field. He was kicking a ball around with Kevin Camilleri and Mandy Banks. George Brennan and Manny Gonzalez were on the swings, laughing at something.

Probably at one of George's jokes.

Everyone was having a great time.

The strange thing was, the only kids on the playground were the kids in class 3A. Everyone else had already gone in to start the school day. But no one had told the kids in Katie's class to stop playing and come inside.

"I wonder where Mrs. Derkman is?" Becky asked.

Usually, their teacher was on the playground before school began. When it was time for classes to start, she would blow her whistle, and the kids would line up to go into the building. But, this morning, Mrs. Derkman was nowhere to be found.

"Do you think we should go inside on our own?" Katie wondered. "School started five minutes ago."

"No way," Suzanne said between jumps. "I'm not going in there until someone tells me I have to."

Just then, Mr. Kane, the school principal, strolled onto the playground. "Class 3A," he called out. "You need to be in school now. Line up."

Katie immediately dropped her end of the double-Dutch ropes, and ran for the door. Suzanne tripped over the fallen ropes. *Plop.* She landed right on her rear end.

"Nice one, Suzanne," George Brennan teased. "How about giving us an instant replay?" He raced past her.

Suzanne glared at George.

As the kids lined up, Jeremy turned to Katie. "Do you think Mrs. Derkman is absent today?" he asked her.

Katie shook her head. "No way. Mrs. Derkman is *never* absent."

"I know," George agreed. "She's *always* at school. She's here when we get here in the morning, and she's here when we leave in the afternoon. I'd swear she lived in the school—if I didn't know she'd moved in next door to you, Katie Kazoo."

The other kids all looked sympathetically at Katie. Imagine having your teacher live right next door. Especially a strict teacher like Mrs. Derkman. Talk about bad luck!

"Maybe she's preparing a surprise for us in the classroom," Miriam Chan suggested.

"Oh, that would be awful," George moaned.

"How do you know?" Miriam asked him. "It could be something great."

"Any surprise Mrs. *Jerk*man could dream up would have to be bad," George told her. George did not like Mrs. Derkman very much.

"You children keep quiet as you walk down the hall," Mr. Kane warned as he led them inside. "The other classes are already busy learning."

$$\times \quad \times \quad \times$$

Sure enough, Mrs. Derkman was there when the kids walked into the room. She was standing in the back of the room, looking through the lens of a video camera. The camera was planted firmly on top of a stand.

"What's that for?" Manny asked Mrs. Derkman.

"I'm going to tape our day," Mrs. Derkman explained.

"Why?" Manny asked.

Mrs. Derkman checked the lens one more time, and then walked to the front of the

room. "After school, I'm going to watch the tapes to see how I teach. That way, I can study what I'm doing right, and what I'm doing wrong. I can come up with ways to be a better teacher."

Katie looked at George. She could tell by the expression on his face that he was practically bursting with ideas for how Mrs. Derkman could be a better teacher. He opened his mouth to say something, but Mrs. Derkman shot him a look. George kept quiet.

"So you're going to watch the tapes the way a coach does after a football game, to see where the team went wrong," Jeremy said.

"Exactly," Mrs. Derkman told him. "You see, I've been entered in the Cherrydale Teacher of the Year Contest. One of the judges is going to come here and watch me teach. I want to make sure that I do my best."

"When is the judge coming?" Kevin asked.

Mrs. Derkman shrugged. "It's a surprise. I don't know when he will come or what he will grade me on."

The kids all stared at their teacher with amazement. Someone was going to give Mrs. Derkman a grade? Now that was a switch!

Mrs. Derkman walked over to the board and picked up a piece of chalk. "Now, just forget about the camera. Pretend it's not there. We have work to do."

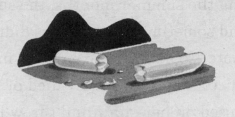

# Chapter 2

Mrs. Derkman may not have wanted anyone to think about the camera, but the kids couldn't help it. In fact, it was *all* they could think about.

"Who can tell me one problem the pioneers faced on their trip out west?" Mrs. Derkman asked the class during social studies. Many hands shot up. "Suzanne?" Mrs. Derkman said.

Usually, Suzanne would just give her answer from her seat. But not today. Suzanne stood up. She turned her face to the video camera, reached up, and wiped her forehead. Then she clutched her throat like she was in pain.

"During the summer months, the sun was strong, and sometimes the settlers didn't have enough water to drink," she moaned in a pained voice. "People actually died of thirst." She collapsed on her chair and threw her head back, pretending to faint.

The class began to laugh. A few kids actually applauded. Suzanne stood up and bowed.

"Watch out, Suzanne Superstar is ready for her close-up," Kevin teased.

"Suzanne, sit down," Mrs. Derkman said with a sigh. She looked at the class. "That's true. Both food and water were hard to come by. Now, does anyone else have a thought?"

Katie had some ideas about what problems the pioneers might have had. But she didn't raise her hand. She didn't want to risk giving a wrong answer. If she did, it would be on film forever!

But George wasn't afraid to be on camera. He raised his hand high.

Mrs. Derkman looked around the room to

see if anyone else had a hand up. But George was the only one. "George," Mrs. Derkman said finally.

Like Suzanne, George stood up and turned toward the camera. He held his pencil in his hand, and pretended it was a microphone. "Speaking of westward travel," he said. "Do you know why a drama teacher is like the pony express? Because he's a stage coach!"

A few kids laughed.

"Does anyone know who settled in the west before anyone else?" George continued.

"Who?" Manny asked.

"The sun!" George exclaimed.

The kids all laughed. "Tell another one, George," Kevin shouted.

George grinned. "Why did the criminal carry glue with him when he traveled out west?"

"Why?" Kevin shouted out.

"He wanted to stick up the passengers!"

Everyone laughed . . . everyone but Mrs.

Derkman, that is. "George, this is a classroom, not a comedy club," she scolded.

Mrs. Derkman did not look happy. Her face was all scrunched up, her glasses were halfway down her nose, and she'd squeezed her fist so tight that she'd snapped the chalk in half.

Katie glanced at the video camera in the back of the room. *I wonder how Mrs. Derkman will feel when she sees herself looking like that,* she thought to herself.

Mrs. Derkman didn't turn off her video camera at all during the day. And the more the camera recorded her, the stricter she got. During math time, the kids were all answering multiplication problems in their notebooks. Mrs. Derkman walked around the room, checking their work.

"Mandy, you know that by third grade all of your work has to be written in cursive," Mrs. Derkman scolded her.

Mandy seemed confused. "But this is math," she told her teacher. "There's no such thing as a cursive 7."

Mrs. Derkman continued walking around the room. She stopped in front of the third row. "Class, what is the rule about eating in this room?"

Katie looked around. She didn't see anyone eating anything.

"There is *no* eating in this classroom," Mrs. Derkman said, answering her own question. She strutted over to the window, and stared at

Speedy. "You've been here long enough to know that," she scolded the hamster.

Speedy took one look at Mrs. Derkman's angry face, and leaped away from his food bowl. He ran to hide inside his plastic tube.

The kids stared at their teacher. Worrying about the contest had obviously made her nuts!

"Boy, Mrs. Derkman is in a really bad mood today," Katie whispered to Kevin and Suzanne.

"I'll say," Suzanne agreed. "I think it has to do with that video camera. Some people act strange when there's a camera around."

Katie looked at "Suzanne Superstar" and laughed. "Gee, you think so?"

# Chapter 3

Mrs. Derkman finally turned off her camera just before the bell rang. She relaxed right away. So did the kids. "Okay, children," the teacher said, a slight smile returning to her face. "Jeremy is now going to pass out this week's edition of the *Class 3A Times*."

Jeremy stood and proudly began to hand out the newspapers. He really loved being the editor of the class newspaper. "There are lots of great articles this week," he told the other kids. "Like the one about . . ."

"*My* new column is in there," Suzanne interrupted him. "It's called 'Ask Suzanne.' I know everyone is going to love it."

"I can't think of anything I'd want to ask her," Kevin whispered to George.

"I can," George answered. "I want to ask her to go away." Kevin and George laughed.

Suzanne scowled at them. "Shows what you know. I'm going to answer very important questions in my column. This week, I wrote about friendship."

Katie watched as Suzanne argued with

George and Kevin. "Are you sure giving Suzanne her own column was a good idea?" she whispered to Jeremy.

"I needed another article to fill the page," Jeremy admitted.

"But you know Suzanne. This could be trouble," Katie told him.

"It'll be okay," Jeremy answered. "Actually, her advice was pretty good. Read it."

Katie opened the newspaper to page three. Suzanne's column was at the top of the page. The question was:

*Dear Suzanne,*

*My friend has a pair of pants that she loves to wear. But they are too tight and short on her, and I'm afraid they will split open! I want to tell her, but I don't want her to get mad at me.*

*Signed,*

*What Do I Do?*

Suzanne had answered:

*Dear What Do I Do?:*
*You should definitely tell your friend that*
*her pants are too small. What if they split in*
*the middle of recess? You will save her from*
*embarrassment. Friends should always be*
*honest with each other. When it comes to*
*friendship, honesty is always the best policy.*

"You see," Jeremy said after Katie had
read the column. "Suzanne said people
should be honest. What trouble could that
cause?"

Katie shrugged. "I guess you're right," she
agreed.

✕ ✕ ✕

That afternoon, Katie went home and did
her homework. Then she went out into her
yard to look for her cocker spaniel, Pepper.
She found him next door, playing with Mrs.
Derkman's dog, Snowball. They were both

sniffing around the tomatoes and cucumbers in Mrs. Derkman's yard.

Katie figured Mrs. Derkman must not be in the yard. Otherwise, she would have shooed the dogs away from her vegetables. Mrs. Derkman loved her garden. She treated her plants like babies. She even sang to them!

Katie was right, Mrs. Derkman wasn't in the garden. But *Mr.* Derkman was. Katie was very surprised. She'd never seen her teacher's husband working in the garden before. He liked to lie in a big hammock under the tree while his wife dug up weeds and planted flowers. But, today, he was the one out there picking fresh cucumbers from the vine.

"Hi, Katie," Mr. Derkman greeted her.

"Hi," Katie replied. "I didn't know you liked to garden."

"I don't," Mr. Derkman admitted. "But my wife is so busy watching her videotapes that she doesn't have time to pick vegetables.

These cucumbers will rot on the vine if I don't bring them in."

"Mrs. Derkman sure is excited about the Teacher of the Year Contest," Katie said.

"I know," Mr. Derkman agreed. "I don't think I've ever seen her this way before. She says if she had only one wish, it would be to win Teacher of the Year."

Katie gulped slightly when Mr. Derkman said that. She knew a lot about wishes. Sometimes, when they came true, they caused a lot of trouble.

Katie learned all about wishes one evening after she'd had a really bad day. She'd lost the football game for her team, ruined her favorite pair of pants, and let out a big burp in front of the whole class. That night, Katie had wished she could be anyone but herself.

There must have been a shooting star overhead when she made that wish, because the very next day, the magic wind came and

turned Katie into Speedy the class hamster!
All morning long, she gnawed on chew sticks
and ran on a hamster wheel, until she finally
turned back into herself!

The magic wind continued to come back
again and again. It had already turned Katie
into other kids, like Suzanne's baby sister
Heather, and her friends Becky Stern and
Jeremy Fox. Another time, it turned her into
her dog Pepper—and she'd gotten into a huge
argument with a particularly nasty squirrel.
Once, the wind even turned her into Mr.
Kane, the school principal. The whole school
was almost destroyed that time!

Katie never knew when the magic wind
would come back again. All she knew was
that when it did, she was going to wind up
getting into some sort of trouble—and so
would the person or animal she turned into.

That was why Katie knew it was important
to be careful what you wished for!

"Freddy Bear, you have a phone call," Mrs.

Derkman called suddenly from the front door.

Mr. Derkman looked up. "Coming, Snookums," he called back. He turned to Katie. "See you later, kiddo."

Katie sighed as Freddy Bear walked up to the house and went inside with his Snookums. She was *never* going to get used to having Mrs. Derkman as a next-door neighbor.

# Chapter 4

"Are you sure it's safe to play in your yard today?" Suzanne asked Katie as they left school with Jeremy and George at the end of the next day. "I don't want to run into Mrs. Derkman."

"Mrs. Derkman's not going to be home yet," Katie assured Suzanne. "And when she does get home, she's not going to bother us. She'll be spending all her time inside watching her videotapes."

"I hope you're right," Jeremy said. "I don't like playing at your house very much now that Mrs. Derkman is your neighbor. I see enough of her at school."

Katie frowned. It made her feel bad that her best friend didn't want to play at her house.

"I was just being honest," Jeremy told her.

The kids began to walk in the direction of Katie's house. A minute later, Becky came up behind them.

Katie jumped. "Becky, you surprised me," Katie exclaimed.

"She didn't surprise *me*," Suzanne said. "She always shows up when Jeremy's around."

Jeremy and Becky both blushed. Then Jeremy looked angry.

"What?" Suzanne asked. "I was just being honest."

Jeremy scowled at Suzanne, but said nothing. What could he say? He was the editor of the class paper. It had been his idea to print Suzanne's advice column in the first place.

"Hi, kids," Mrs. Carew greeted them as they walked up the walkway to Katie's house.

"I hope you're hungry. I've got lots of chocolate chip cookies." She held out a large plate.

Becky grabbed a chocolate chip cookie and took a bite. "This is pretty good, Mrs. Carew," she said. "But my mom makes them much better. Hers are chewier, and they have a lot more chips."

Katie's mom didn't know what to say. The kids all stared at Becky with surprise.

Becky shrugged. "I was just being . . ."

"Honest," George, Jeremy, Suzanne, and Katie finished her sentence for her.

The other kids seemed to like the cookies a lot. They chowed down on them. When they were finished eating, Katie's mom took the empty plate into the house. "Don't stay out here too long," she warned Katie as she went inside. "You have to do your homework."

Katie nodded. "We don't have too much," she assured her mother.

"Does anyone else think Mrs. Derkman is acting especially weird lately?" Suzanne asked the others once Mrs. Carew was gone and they were alone.

"I'll say," Becky agreed. "Did you hear her yelling at Speedy yesterday?"

"Poor little hamster," Katie agreed.

George stood up. He wrinkled his brow and scrunched up his mouth. He pretended to look through a pair of glasses.

"Speedy, there will be no scratching in this classroom," he said, imitating Mrs. Derkman. "And there will be no running on the hamster wheel. There is no running in the classroom at all. Save that for the playground."

Katie giggled.

"No laughing, Katie," George said in a stern voice. "School is not supposed to be fun."

"It sure wasn't fun today," Jeremy said. "I was afraid to breathe."

"That's the new rule," George said. "From now on, students are only allowed to breathe during lunch."

The kids all laughed. George was imitating their teacher perfectly.

"That's pretty good, George," Jeremy giggled.

"Yeah, you sound just like Mrs. *Jerk*man," Suzanne agreed.

Suddenly, the kids heard footsteps on the sidewalk. They stopped laughing and turned around.

"Uh-oh," Becky murmured.

Mrs. Derkman was standing in her driveway. She had just arrived home from school. Katie was sure her teacher had heard them talking about her.

"We're in trouble now," George whispered.

But Mrs. Derkman didn't say a word. She just turned, and sadly went into her house.

# Chapter 5

When Katie arrived at school the next morning, everyone was upset. And not because of how strict Mrs. Derkman had become. The kids were fighting with one another—and it was all because of Suzanne's advice column.

"I don't know what your problem is," Katie heard Jeremy say to Manny. "All I said was that you don't run fast enough to be on our team in the relay race."

"That's really mean," Manny replied.

"I'm just being honest," Jeremy told him. "You're not a fast runner. As your friend, I owe it to you to tell you the truth."

Jeremy and Manny weren't the only ones having an argument. George and Kevin weren't getting along too well, either.

"Here's my new joke," George said. "What do you call a jogging almond?"

"What?" Kevin asked.

"A health nut!" George laughed, but Kevin didn't.

George looked at him strangely. "Don't you get it?"

Kevin nodded. "I get it. I just don't think it's funny."

George's eyes opened wide. "What do you mean it's not funny?" he demanded.

"Hey, don't get mad at me," Kevin insisted. "I'm just being honest."

George stormed away.

It wasn't only the boys who were having trouble with the truth. As she turned away from George, Katie spotted Zoe Canter sitting under a tree. She was crying. Katie walked over to see what was wrong.

"What's up, Zoe?" she asked.

"Miriam and Mandy just told me not to meet them at the mall on Saturday," Zoe told Katie between sobs.

"Why would they do that?"

Zoe shrugged. "They said they *honestly* wanted some time alone. Now *I* have nothing to do. I can't believe they're leaving me out like this."

Katie sighed. The kids were taking Suzanne's advice too seriously. Sometimes, the truth hurt. Katie decided to talk to Suzanne about it. Maybe her friend could write a new article for next week's paper— one that was about not hurting other people's feelings.

But, before Katie could speak to Suzanne, Mrs. Derkman blew her whistle three times. It was time to go inside.

The kids were still arguing as they walked into the classroom, put their homework in the bin, and hung up their jackets. As soon as everyone was in their seats, Mrs. Derkman called for quiet.

"You have to be especially well-behaved now," Mrs. Derkman reminded the class. "The judges for the Teacher of the Year Contest will be here any day now. It could be today, tomorrow, or the next day."

"You mean we have to be good for three whole days?" George asked. "I don't know if I can do that."

Mrs. Derkman didn't say anything. She didn't have to. The look on her face was enough to make George be quiet.

"She's in a bad mood again!" Suzanne mumbled under her breath.

Unfortunately, she wasn't so quiet that Mrs. Derkman couldn't hear her. The teacher's face got even more angry. She stared at the second row. "Did you say something . . . Katie?" she asked.

"No," Katie assured her honestly.

"Yes, you did," Mrs. Derkman said. "I heard you."

"It wasn't me," Katie insisted. "It was . . ." Katie stopped herself. She didn't want to squeal on Suzanne.

"There is no rudeness allowed in this class. Go down and sit in Mr. Kane's office," Mrs. Derkman told her. "You need to spend some time thinking about how your words affect others."

"But I . . ."

"No buts, Katie. I said go to Mr. Kane's office."

Katie could feel tears welling up in her eyes. She was being punished, and she hadn't done anything wrong. That was the worst feeling in the world.

The hallway was empty as Katie made her way toward the principal's office. Suddenly, she felt a cool, gentle breeze blowing on the back of her neck. She looked up to see if a window was open. But all the windows in the hallway were shut tight. So were the doors. The breeze wasn't coming from outside.

Oh, no! The magic wind was back!

Within seconds, the wind began to swirl around Katie like a wild tornado, blowing her hair all around her face. Katie shut her eyes tight. The wind grew stronger—so strong that Katie thought it would blow her away!

And then it stopped. Just like that. The magic wind was gone.

Which could only mean one thing. Katie had turned into someone else. The question was, who?

# Chapter 6

"What page should we turn to, Mrs. Derkman?" Katie heard someone ask.

Slowly, she opened her eyes. She looked around. The room was very familiar. There was a hamster by the window, rows of desks, and a bulletin board that said "Math Rules!" on the back wall.

Katie knew this classroom very well. This was her classroom. Class 3A.

Okay, so now she knew where she was. But she didn't know *who* she was.

"Mrs. Derkman," Mandy said again. "You didn't tell us what page to turn to."

All eyes seemed to be on Katie. Katie looked down at the floor. There were sensible

leather shoes on her feet. She was wearing a
black skirt that just covered her knees, and a
long-sleeved white blouse. Katie would never
wear boring clothes like that.

But Mrs. Derkman would!

Oh, no! Katie had turned into her teacher!

Katie gulped. She didn't know anything about being a teacher. She didn't even know what book the kids had on their desks. She'd been in the hall when Mrs. Derkman had started the lesson.

But there was one person who knew how to be Mrs. Derkman. And he did it perfectly. Katie thought back to yesterday, when George had imitated Mrs. Derkman. She tried to do what he had done. She wrinkled her brow, and scrunched up her mouth. She looked down through Mrs. Derkman's half-glasses.

"Mrs. Derkman, do you have a toothache?" Miriam Chan asked her.

Katie sighed. Obviously, she didn't look as much like Mrs. Derkman as she'd thought. She was never going to be able to teach her friends anything.

But she had to do *something* with the class. Otherwise, they were sure to figure out that she wasn't really their teacher. Katie thought for a moment. Then she came up with a plan.

"Class, I've changed my mind," Katie said finally. "We're going to start the day with free reading. Everyone, take out your books."

The kids all looked at one another. They never started the day with free reading.

"What are you waiting for?" Katie scolded them, trying to sound like Mrs. Derkman. "Take out your books."

The kids did as they were told. As they began to read, Katie sat down at Mrs. Derkman's desk. The blue notebook Mrs. Derkman always carried was sitting right there. Maybe there was some clue in there about what Mrs. Derkman had wanted to teach today.

Katie opened the notebook. On the first page was a list of the kids in class 3A. Next to each of the names was a row of letters. She looked at the first one.

*Kevin Camilleri: B, B+, A, C*

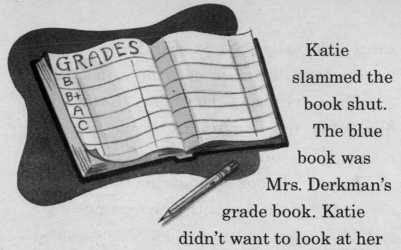

Katie slammed the book shut. The blue book was Mrs. Derkman's grade book. Katie didn't want to look at her friends' test grades. Well, maybe she *wanted* to, but she knew she shouldn't. Grades were private.

Katie sat back in Mrs. Derkman's big, wooden chair and sighed. Her only hope was that the magic wind would blow again and turn her back into herself before she actually had to teach anything.

The trouble with that plan was that the magic wind only came when Katie was alone. Teachers were never alone in school. There were always kids around them. Teachers never even got to go to the bathroom. At least, Katie had never seen one get up to go.

As Katie thought about her big problem, she heard whispering. She looked out at her friends. Becky was whispering something to Jeremy.

"Becky!" Katie scolded her, trying to sound like their teacher. "We are reading now."

Becky looked back down at her book.

One minute later, Katie watched as a note flew across the room and landed on Zoe's desk. Katie knew that Mrs. Derkman would take the note and read it out loud. But Katie couldn't be that mean.

"Zoe, throw that in the garbage right now," she said instead.

Zoe stood up and did as she was told.

After that, everyone was quiet. At least for a few minutes. Then Kevin started drumming his fingers on his desk. *Tap tap tap. Tap tap tap.*

George began humming as he read. *Hmmm. Hmmm. Hmmm.*

The sound was driving Katie crazy. "Kevin! George!" she shouted, her voice suddenly sounding shrill and sharp. "This isn't music class. There's no singing or drumming here. You need to be quiet."

"Boy, Mrs. *Jerk*man is really mean today," Mandy whispered to Suzanne.

Katie frowned. She hadn't been trying to be mean. She'd just been trying to make sure everyone could read. Obviously, free reading time wasn't working. Katie was going to have to teach a lesson whether she liked it or not.

She wrote a division problem on the board.

$$3\overline{)15}$$

"Okay, class, put away your books," Katie said. "We're going to have a math lesson. Today, we will review division."

It was better to review something than to teach something new. After all, Katie didn't know anything new.

"Fifteen divided by three is five," Jeremy said.

"Very good," Katie agreed.

"That's not good," Suzanne interrupted.

"It's not?" Katie asked her.

"No. He called out. We're not allowed to call out," Suzanne explained.

*Oops.* Suzanne was right. Mrs. Derkman did not allow anyone to answer a question without raising his or her hand.

"So what?" Becky butted in. "He was right, wasn't he?"

"But he didn't follow the rules," Suzanne said.

"Well, neither did you," Jeremy told her. "You just called out, too."

Before Katie could say anything, Mr. Kane entered the room. He was followed by a stranger in a blue suit. The stranger was carrying a notebook. The two men walked quietly to the back of the room. Mr. Kane smiled and whispered something to the visitor.

Suddenly, Katie had a horrible thought. The stranger must be the judge for the Teacher of the Year Contest. He was going to judge Mrs. Derkman right now. And Mrs. Derkman wasn't even there!

This was *so* not good.

# Chapter 7

There was nothing Katie could do but keep on teaching. Quickly, she scribbled another division problem on the board.

"Who can answer this question?" Katie asked the class. "What is twenty-seven divided by nine?" Lots of kids raised their hands. "Kevin?" Katie said.

"Four," Kevin said confidently.

Katie nodded and turned to the blackboard. She began to write another problem on the board.

But, before she could, Mandy raised her hand. "Mrs. Derkman?"

"Yes, Mandy?" Katie asked.

"Kevin's not right," Mandy told her. "Twenty-seven divided by nine equals three."

"It does not," Kevin argued.

"Sure it does," Mandy told him. "Because nine times three equals twenty-seven."

"Uh, very good, Mandy. I must have heard Kevin incorrectly," muttered Katie.

Mandy smiled at Katie. "I know all my times tables perfectly, Mrs. Derkman."

"You're stuck-up," Kevin said.

"That's not nice," Miriam chimed in.

"I'm just being honest, like Suzanne said we should be," Kevin told her.

"You're jealous because I'm better in math and sports than you are," Mandy told him.

"You're not so great, Mandy," Becky butted in. "You're not the best soccer player in the class. Jeremy is. And that's the honest truth!"

Katie knew she had to calm the kids down. But how? "You guys, come on," she said helplessly.

No one listened to her. Instead, the

arguing got worse. "Becky, you always say things like that," Suzanne said. "Everyone knows you have a big, fat crush on Jeremy."

Jeremy blushed. He turned to Suzanne. "Well, as long as we're being honest," he said, "you look like a banana in that yellow dress!"

Suzanne gulped. No one had ever said anything bad about her clothes before. "I do not!" she shouted. "This is a very cool outfit. Everybody thinks so."

"I don't," Becky said. "I think Jeremy is right. You *do* look like a banana."

"You don't know anything about style," Suzanne shouted back.

"You think you're the best at everything," Becky said to Suzanne.

"I do not!" Suzanne shouted back.

"I'm just telling the truth," Becky said. "But you're not the best. Can you do this?" Becky leaped out of her seat and did a back flip. She landed on the floor in a split.

Katie looked helplessly at the class. She

gulped. Mr. Kane was still standing there in the back of the room. But he didn't look happy anymore. His face was beet red, and his eyes were bulging. A vein was throbbing at the top of his bald head.

The principal couldn't take the arguing anymore. He took a step toward the front of the room and opened his mouth to speak.

But, before Mr. Kane could say a word, the judge tapped him on the shoulder. He whispered something in the principal's ear. Mr. Kane whispered something back. The judge shook his head.

Mr. Kane threw his hands up in the air. "This is a disaster!" he said. Then he stormed out of the room. The door slammed shut behind him.

The judge did not leave the room. He stayed to watch what would happen next. From the look on his face, Katie could tell he was very disappointed at the way things were going. So, Katie did a very un-Derkman thing.

She leaped up on a desk and whistled—loud.

The kids stopped talking and stared at their teacher. Mrs. Derkman had never done anything like that before.

"Okay, everyone sit down," Katie said. "This is not a nice way to act."

"But we're just being honest," Suzanne said. "Friends have to be honest with each other."

Katie nodded. "There's a difference between being honest, and being mean," she said. "I think maybe you were using Suzanne's advice column as an excuse to be mean. And that is totally not okay."

*Totally not okay?* The kids all stared at one another. Mrs. Derkman never spoke like that.

"I think it's okay to be honest if you're trying to help someone. But you should do that in private. And sometimes it's better to keep quiet than to say something that'll hurt your friend's feelings. You guys didn't care whose feelings you hurt."

The class stared at her. Mrs. Derkman never called her class *you guys*. She always called them children or students. Mrs. Derkman sure was acting strange.

But she was right. And the kids knew it.

At first, no one said anything. Then, Mandy turned to Kevin. "I guess it wasn't nice to say you weren't good in math or sports. You're really good at basketball."

Kevin nodded. "Thanks. And you're amazing in math. I guess I was just mad that I got the problem wrong."

Katie smiled at the class. "I think we should put our math books away. I have a better lesson." She began to hand out pieces of paper. "I want each of you to make a list of everyone in this class. Then I want you to write one nice thing about each of your class-mates."

"I'll start with George. He's really funny," Jeremy said as he began his list.

"Suzanne has great style," Becky said, writing on her paper. "And Jeremy is an awesome soccer player."

"Zoe is a terrific artist," Miriam added as she wrote.

"Manny has good handwriting," Suzanne murmured as she began to make up her list.

Before long, the kids were all busy writing. Katie looked back at the contest judge. He seemed really happy to see the students interested in their work!

But would that be enough for Mrs. Derkman to win the contest?

# Chapter 8

Somehow, Katie managed to get through the rest of the day as Mrs. Derkman. When school ended, she was really tired. Keeping a whole class of third-graders busy and out of trouble wasn't easy. Katie just wanted to go home and relax.

But which home should she go to? She couldn't go to her house. Not as long as she looked like Mrs. Derkman. As she walked home, Katie began to worry. This was the longest she'd ever spent as someone else.

Katie hoped the magic wind would come back soon. If it didn't, Katie might wind up eating dinner with Freddy Bear Derkman!

Just then, the door to Mrs. Derkman's house swung open. But it wasn't the magic wind that did it. It was Mr. Derkman.

"Surprise, Snookums," he called out as he walked toward Katie. "I got out of work early."

"Oh, hello, Mr. Derk . . ." Katie began. "I mean, Freddy Bear."

Mr. Derkman reached out his arms. "How about a kissy-poo, Snookums?" he asked. He puckered up his lips for a big smooch.

*Yuck!* Katie certainly didn't want to give Freddy Bear a kissy-poo! But how could she avoid it?

"Ruff! Ruff!" Just then, Pepper came running over to Katie. He rubbed his back up against her knees and barked happily. Katie bent down and scratched him gratefully behind the ears.

Pepper licked Katie on the nose. He knew she wasn't *really* Mrs. Derkman. Pepper would know his Katie anywhere.

But Snowball didn't know who Katie was. She ran up and sniffed at Katie. Then she looked up, confused. This person looked like her human mommy, she smelled like her human mommy, but somehow Snowball knew that she wasn't Mrs. Derkman. Snowball began to bark wildly.

"I guess she's hungry," Mr. Derkman said. "I'll take her inside and give her some food."

As Mr. Derkman went back into the house, Katie breathed a sigh of relief. Thank goodness for dogs. But Katie knew she couldn't avoid kissing Mr. Derkman forever—at least not as long as she was *Mrs.* Derkman.

Just then, Katie felt a cool breeze blowing on the back of her neck. Katie looked up at the trees. The leaves were still. She looked down at the grass. Not a blade was moving.

The magic wind was back.

Within seconds, the wind was swirling around her like a giant tornado. Katie felt like she could be blown away at any minute. Quickly, she grabbed onto a tree and shut her eyes, tight.

And then it stopped. Just like that.

Slowly, Katie opened her eyes. She looked down at her feet. The sensible leather shoes were gone, and there were platform sneakers in their place. Instead of a skirt, Katie was wearing jeans, with laces down the sides. She put her hands to her face. She wasn't wearing glasses anymore.

Just then, Katie's mother came outside.

"There you are, Katie," her mother said. "How was school?"

Katie smiled brightly. She was back! "School was okay," she said.

"Anything exciting happen?"

Katie knew she couldn't tell her mother what had happened today. Her mother wouldn't believe her. Katie wouldn't have believed it either, if it hadn't happened to her.

"Nah," Katie said finally. "It was just a regular day."

# Chapter 9

Most of the kids in class 3A were already on the playground by the time Katie arrived at school the next day. But they weren't playing or running around. They were busy watching as Mr. Kane spoke to Mrs. Derkman. The principal did not look happy.

"Your class was out of control yesterday," he told Mrs. Derkman.

"I know," Mrs. Derkman admitted sadly. "I'm not sure how that happened."

"What do you mean?" Mr. Kane asked.

"Well, I mean, I know what happened. But it's almost like that wasn't me up there in the front of the room." Mrs. Derkman sounded very confused.

"It certainly looked like you," Mr. Kane told her.

"It was me," Mrs. Derkman said. "I mean, at least I think it was. But I didn't feel like me. Oh, I don't know what to think."

Mr. Kane shook his head. "Well, it doesn't matter now. It doesn't seem as though you'll be winning the Teacher of the Year Award this time around."

Mrs. Derkman looked like she was about to cry.

✕   ✕   ✕

"Boy, Mrs. Jerkman looks unhappy. Mr. Kane must be really mad at her," George told the other kids.

"That's not nice, George," Katie said.

"What?" George asked her.

"Calling her Mrs. Jerkman," Katie told him.

"We always call her that," Kevin said.

"It's still not nice."

The other kids stared at Katie. *Was she*

*really standing up for their teacher?*

"Mrs. Derkman isn't nice to us, either," Suzanne reminded Katie. "She's very strict. And she gets mad a lot."

"That's because we're not always very good in class," Katie reminded her. "We pass notes and whisper."

"Yeah, well, Mrs. Derkman writes notes, too," George argued. "She sent one to my mother last week. And it wasn't a nice note, either!"

Katie rolled her eyes. "What about yesterday?" she asked the kids. "Everybody was yelling at each other during math. The judge from that contest saw the whole fight."

"How do you know what happened?" George asked Katie. "You were in Mr. Kane's office all day."

Of course, Katie *had* been in the classroom. But she couldn't tell the other kids that. So, instead, she said, "I heard about it. It sounds like everyone was mad at each other."

"But we made up," Mandy told Katie. "And we wrote nice things about each other. The judge from the contest saw us doing that, too."

"Yeah, he seemed happy about that," Miriam added. "He was really smiling when he left."

Katie shrugged. "But he wasn't happy enough to make Mrs. Derkman the Teacher of the Year. She really wanted that award. We blew it for her."

"She blew it for herself," George said. "She jumped up on a desk and whistled. If I did that, she'd send me to the principal's office."

"Yeah," Kevin agreed.

Katie gulped. George was right. Maybe if she hadn't jumped up on that desk, Mrs. Derkman would have had a chance. Now Katie felt worse than ever. "Mrs. Derkman deserves that award. She works really hard. Her feet hurt at the end of the day," Katie insisted.

Jeremy looked at her strangely. "How do you know?" he asked.

"I . . . er . . . well, she stands up at the board so much, I just figure they would hurt," Katie said quickly. "Besides, Mrs. Derkman might not be the nicest teacher in the school, but we learn a lot with her. We're the only class who studied geography this year. And we're the only ones who got to do research projects on things that interested us."

The kids couldn't argue with that. They *had* learned a lot in third grade. For a minute, everyone was quiet.

"We should make it up to her," Mandy said finally.

"I'm going to try to be extra good today," Miriam vowed.

"Me, too," Zoe agreed.

"I guess I will, too," Kevin said. He turned to Suzanne. "That means you can't ask me to pass any notes to Katie."

"I won't," Suzanne agreed. "I'm not going to write any notes today."

It sounded like everyone was going to try to make Mrs. Derkman happy today. Everyone except George, that is. He hadn't said anything about being good in class. All the kids turned to look at him.

"Why are you all staring at me?" George asked.

"Because we want you to be nice to Mrs. Derkman today," said Miriam.

"Yeah," agreed Zoe.

"That means no jokes, George," Kevin said, laughing.

"Oh, boy," replied George.

"George, please be nice to Mrs. Derkman today," Katie pleaded.

George sighed. "Do I have to?"

"Come on, George," Kevin said. "If I have to be good, so do you. Besides, it will really freak her out if *you're* good."

George smiled brightly. He liked that idea.

"Okay," he agreed. "But just for today."

Katie looked at her friends and grinned. Mrs. Derkman wasn't going to get a big trophy. But she was going to have an easy day teaching class 3A. Surely that would make her happy.

# Chapter 10

The kids were all true to their word. No one spoke without raising their hand. No one passed any notes in class. No one chewed gum, or stared at the clock, or doodled in their notebook.

But Mrs. Derkman didn't seem to notice how well her students were behaving. She just frowned and sighed a lot.

At the end of the day, Mrs. Derkman told the kids to open their free reading books. Usually, Mrs. Derkman watched the kids as they read to make sure no one misbehaved. But today, Mrs. Derkman stared out the window. She didn't seem to notice the class at all.

Suddenly, there was a knock at the door. Mr. Kane walked into the classroom. He was carrying a gold trophy.

Mrs. Derkman turned and looked at him in confusion. "What is this for?" she asked. "I don't understand."

"This is for you," Mr. Kane said. "It's from the Cherrydale Teacher of the Year Award Committee."

"But you said I didn't win," Mrs. Derkman reminded him.

"You didn't win Teacher of the Year. That went to a teacher at the middle school."

"Then what is that trophy for?" Mrs. Derkman asked him.

"It's a special award," Mr. Kane said. "It's the first time they've ever given it."

"What's it for?" Katie asked excitedly, forgetting that she wasn't supposed to call out in class.

Mrs. Derkman must have forgotten that rule, too. She didn't yell at Katie. Instead she asked, "Yes, what is it for?"

Mr. Kane looked at the plaque on the base of the trophy. *"This award is presented to Mrs. Barbara Derkman for her creative lesson on consideration and caring for one another's feelings,"* he read.

Katie smiled. She *knew* the judge had liked that part of the class.

Mr. Kane gave Mrs. Derkman her trophy. "The contest judge called to tell me he liked the way you were able to get your students to apologize and see the good in one another," he said. Then he added, "Asking the students to write nice things about each of their classmates was a great idea."

"Oh," Mrs. Derkman said. "I guess you're talking about that pile of papers on my desk."

"You sound like you don't know where those papers came from," Mr. Kane laughed.

Mrs. Derkman didn't say anything. The truth was, she *wasn't* completely sure about anything that had happened yesterday.

"Anyway, he was really impressed with the way you were able to talk to your students on their own level. He said you almost sounded like a third-grader yourself."

Katie choked back a laugh. Mrs. Derkman had sounded like a third-grader yesterday because she *was* a third-grader. But, of course, Katie was the only one who knew that. And she wasn't going to tell anyone.

"I'm sure your class is very proud of you,"

Mr. Kane told Mrs. Derkman. He started to clap for her. The kids clapped, too.

"I'm proud of them," Mrs. Derkman told Mr. Kane. "I may not be the teacher of the year, but 3A is definitely Cherrydale's Class of the Year. To celebrate, I'm not giving any homework today. I want you all to go home and play!"

The class cheered even louder.

"Does this mean we can stop being good now?" George whispered to Katie as the class cheered for their teacher.

Before Katie could answer him, she felt a cool breeze on the back of her neck. *Oh, no! Was the magic wind back again? Was it going to change her into someone else right here in front of all her friends?* The magic wind had never come when other people were around before. But there was a first time for everything.

"Katie, you'd better close that window," Mrs. Derkman said. "That wind isn't good for

Speedy. He might catch a cold."

Katie breathed a sigh of relief. If Mrs. Derkman felt the breeze, then the magic wind hadn't come back. At least not right now. But it could come back anytime, and turn Katie into anyone.

She hurried to close the window. She never knew who the wind might turn her into next. It could turn her into Speedy again! And the last thing Katie would want to be turned into was a hamster with a cold.

For now, though, Katie was herself. And that made her very happy. After all, of all the people the magic wind had turned her into so far, Katie Carew was the one she liked best.

# An Apple for the Teacher

This apple graham cracker snacker is a snack even Mrs. Derkman can't resist.

**You will need:**

2 red delicious apples

1 cup lemon juice

$1/2$ cup chunky peanut butter

2 tablespoons honey

$1/2$ tsp. cinnamon

6 whole graham crackers

A helpful adult

**Here's what you do:** Ask an adult to core the apples and cut each one in half. Then cut each half into three wedges (so you have 12 apple wedges). Dip the wedges in lemon juice to keep them from browning. Place the wedges in a single layer on a microwavable plate or baking dish. Cover the wedges loosely with waxed paper. Ask an adult to microwave the wedges on high for $3\,^1/_2$–4 minutes (until apples are tender). Drain the apples on a paper towel.

In a small bowl, combine the peanut butter, honey, and cinnamon. Snap the graham crackers in half to make 12 squares. Spread a layer of the peanut butter mixture on each of the six graham cracker squares. Top each square with the remaining graham cracker squares to make sandwiches.

Makes six snacks.